D0325840

The Dastardly Murder
of Dirty Pete

THE
DASTARDLY MURDER OF DIRTY PETE

Eth Clifford

Illustrated by George Hughes

Houghton Mifflin Company
Boston

Library of Congress Cataloging in Publication Data
Clifford, Eth, 1915–
The dastardly murder of Dirty Pete.
Summary: While traveling to the west coast, two sisters and their father have many adventures when they get lost and find a ghost town. Sequel to "Help! I'm a Prisoner in the Library."
[1. West (U.S.) — Fiction.   2. Ghost towns — Fiction. 3. Adventure stories] I. Hughes, George, ill. II. Title.
PZ7.C62214Das   [Fic]   81-6316
ISBN 0-395-31671-5   AACR2

Printed in the United States of America
VB 10 9 8

With love to
Esther and Carl
for so many reasons

Contents

1 A Creepy Sign 1

2 The Going-Nowhere Street 12

3 Coming to Get You! 18

4 "Our Fate Is Sealed" 28

5 Beware the Odd-Numbered Doors 36

6 The Legend of the Whispering Ghost 48

7 "So You've Come Back, Black Bart" 58

8 Meet Sourdough Sam 67

9 Looking For Curly 77

10 The Dancing Skeleton 88

11 No Way Out 93

12 And the Wall Came Tumbling Down 102

13 Everybody Explains 110

14 Never Follow a Creepy Sign 116

1

A Creepy Sign

"I told you we took the wrong turn from the very beginning," Mary Rose said to her father. "I told you and told you, Daddy."

Mr. Onetree sighed and then he pressed his lips together in a tight line.

Mary Rose stared down at the map in her lap and thought, "Now I suppose he's mad at me." She turned her head and looked out the car window.

She had thought her father would be proud of the way she had learned to read road maps. Instead, he was angry. "He never gets angry with Jo-Beth," Mary Rose told herself, "and Jo-Beth says the most ridiculous things." Well,

Jo-Beth was his favorite, everybody knew that. He probably liked Jo-Beth even more than the baby, Harry Two, and that was a *lot* because he had always wanted a boy.

Mary Rose made up her mind not to give her father any more directions on this long trip they were taking to the West Coast to visit Grandmother Onetree. Why try to be helpful if he didn't even care?

Still, she couldn't keep from wishing that it was her mother who was doing the driving. Her mother would have followed the road map.

"When I leave Point A, I want to get to Point B by the most direct route." Mrs. Onetree usually looked at her husband when she said this. But Mr. Onetree liked to travel without any set plan. He'd go shooting off the main highways "to see what we can see," he explained. "You never know what you might come across hidden on one of these little side roads."

That was because he was a reporter. And

of course since he got the idea about writing a book on the different kinds of people he met when he was on a trip, it was worse than ever.

Mr. Onetree had made so many turns since they had left the highway that even he had to admit finally that they were lost. That was when Mary Rose had reminded her father that she had "told him and told him."

"Okay, kids," he said, tapping the wheel. "No reason to worry. There has to be a main highway up ahead somewhere. Mary Rose, take another look at the map. See if you can find a heavy black line going west."

Jo-Beth, sitting in the corner of the back seat of the car, had been passing the time meanwhile just lost in daydreams. She was the daughter of the President of the United States, and she had been kidnaped by gypsies. No. She wasn't being kidnaped, she decided. She was gravely ill and was being rushed to the only hospital in the world that could treat her. There were newspaper headlines about her, and stories praising her bravery and sweet nature. No. Maybe she was a great scientist, about to make a discovery that would change the world.

Suddenly Jo-Beth got tired of pretending. She stared out the window at the lengthening shadows.

"There's nothing to look at," she complained. "Doesn't anybody live around here? Suppose we can't find a main highway? Suppose there aren't any motels? Or people? Or anything?"

"Oh, Jo-Beth." Mary Rose turned around to shake her head at her sister. She didn't know how very much she looked and sounded like her mother just then. "Don't start carrying on."

It was too late, of course, because Jo-Beth was caught up again. "We'll die in the desert," she said with relish, "and years from now they'll find our bleached bones and wonder what our terrible fate was."

A delicious shiver started at the bottom of

her spine and ran cold and tingling up to the back of her neck.

"Just our poor bleached bones." She sounded as if she could hardly wait for it to happen.

Mr. Onetree laughed.

"See?" Mary Rose told herself. "He thinks Jo-Beth is funny. I'll bet if I said something silly like that he wouldn't think I was funny."

Mary Rose knew that she and Jo-Beth looked very much alike, with their fine straight brown hair and dark brown eyes and their bright smiles. But that was only on the outside. They were really very different. Of course Mary Rose was ten and a half, while her sister was only seven and a half. Maybe that was why Mary Rose was so sensible, just because she was so much older and responsible. Her mother even trusted her to help out with Harry Two, who wasn't sensible or silly or anything definite yet, since he was only six months old.

Mary Rose sighed. For a moment she

wished she and Jo-Beth had decided to go on the plane with her mother and Harry Two. Mrs. Onetree had refused to take the long trip in the car.

"Not with a *baby*," she had insisted. "Besides, Harry," she had told her husband, "I know you. You'll be chasing after every will-o'-the-wisp."

The girls had been given the choice of flying with their mother or going with their father. Jo-Beth promptly decided she'd rather go by car. She didn't know what a will-o'-the-wisp was — a leprechaun, maybe, or even a Martian — but she wanted to be there when her father caught it. And though Mary Rose didn't say anything, she felt going with her father and sister would probably be more exciting.

Right now she was sure she had made the wrong decision. She looked down at the map, tracing her finger along the darker lines, trying to find the main highway her father was so certain was somewhere ahead.

"I can't even find the road we're on," she said at last. "This road doesn't have a name. Or a number," she added, with exasperation. It was the dumbest thing she had ever heard of, plopping a road down in the middle of nowhere and not even calling it anything.

"I'm surprised at you," Mr. Onetree told her. "What kind of pioneer would you have been? Just think how the pioneers took off in their Conestoga wagons and hit the dusty trails . . ."

"But Daddy," Jo-Beth interrupted. "They had wagon masters. And food," she said gloomily when her stomach began to make odd noises. "We haven't had our supper yet. I'm starved."

Mary Rose turned around and stared at her sister. "That's funny. You ate the last apple in the bag without even asking if anybody else wanted a bite."

Jo-Beth decided not to answer. Instead she

asked her father, "Daddy, can we eat some of your jellybeans?"

Mary Rose and Jo-Beth didn't like jelly-beans nearly as much as chocolate or nuts or popcorn. But Mr. Onetree's sweet tooth was satisfied only by jellybeans. He had started eating them when he had stopped smoking and always had a bag next to his typewriter when he was writing for the newspaper.

Mr. Onetree refused. "Not so close to supper . . ."

"Daddy," Jo-Beth shrieked. She had just caught sight of something out the window. "Back up. We just went past a sign."

Although they had seen no one on this road for miles, Mr. Onetree checked his rear-view mirror before backing up slowly.

"I see it. Stop the car, Daddy." Mary Rose peered at the sign. "I think I'd better get out and read it. It's all faded."

Mary Rose stood for a long time in front of the wooden board nailed to a time-worn post.

She was there so long Jo-Beth began to grumble.

"What does it *say*?"

Mary Rose got back into the car, looking very uneasy. "It says, 'Inn of the Whispering Ghost on Skull Valley Road. Two miles right at the first crossroad ahead.'"

Jo-Beth's eyes widened.

Mary Rose went on, "It's a real creepy sign.

The way the word *ghost* fades away and the letters seem to shiver and disappear."

"I'm not going to any motel called Inn of the Whispering Ghost on something called Skull Valley Road," Jo-Beth announced flatly.

Mr. Onetree was tired of driving. Going to a motel or hotel, taking a shower, and having a hearty supper seemed a great idea to him. He started the car and took off up the road in a burst of speed that made the dust fly from beneath the wheels.

"Inn of the Whispering Ghost." He laughed. "What a name to attract tourists. I hope we can still get a room."

"Maybe it isn't for tourists. Maybe it's for real. Suppose there really and truly is a whispering ghost," Jo-Beth said faintly.

"Then it will be an adventure." Mr. Onetree began to whistle.

Jo-Beth sat way back in her seat.

"What kind of an adventure?" she asked in a very small voice.

Mary Rose stared straight ahead. She wasn't

surprised that Jo-Beth was uneasy because, sensible as Mary Rose was, she too was beginning to get a hollow sinking feeling in the pit of her stomach.

Adventure, their father had said.

But what kind of adventure was waiting for them at the Inn of the Whispering Ghost?

2

The Going-Nowhere Street

Mr. Onetree drove carefully along Skull Valley Road, which wasn't a road at all but a dusty trail that crawled close to a mountain. It was a dull red color that made Jo-Beth think of dried blood.

"Are we going all the way to the top of the mountain?" Mary Rose wanted to know.

It wasn't a mountain, just a hill, her father explained. Jo-Beth, her head hanging out the window, wondered what the difference was. Whatever it was called, it looked high enough to her.

"They probably did some mining here," Mr. Onetree went on, as he tried to keep the car from going off the rough narrow climbing track. "Silver, maybe. Or even gold."

"I'm not hungry anymore. Honestly, Daddy. Let's go back."

"How can Daddy turn around when he hardly has enough room to drive forward?" Mary Rose asked.

"Let's just wait and see what we find at the end of the road. Maybe this is just part of the atmosphere," Mr. Onetree said.

"What's atmosphere?"

Mr. Onetree shook his head. "I shouldn't expect a seven-year-old to know . . ."

"Seven-and-a-half," said Jo-Beth with great dignity.

"Atmosphere is what sets up the scene for what's going to happen next . . ."

"I know," Mary Rose interrupted. "Like people coming up to a haunted house late at night, and there's thunder and lightning. And all the doors squeak. And the lights are always going out."

Mr. Onetree didn't answer, because they

had reached the end of the trail.

"Daddy, don't forget to put the emergency brake on," Mary Rose warned. "We're on a hill, you know."

But her father had already leaped out of the car and was looking around. The girls tumbled out after him. What they saw made Jo-Beth want to get back in the car as soon as she got out. It made Mary Rose swallow hard.

A group of wooden houses were crowded together. Because of the way the street slanted, the buildings seemed to be leaning against one another. They were gray and shabby and worn, huddled back against the mountain as if afraid to be seen.

Mary Rose could read the faded signs on the stores. MADAM MARGO'S MILLINERY. FENTON'S FEED AND GENERAL STORE. SKULL VALLEY STAGE LINE. BLACK BART'S SALOON. Down toward the middle of the street, the sign on a two-story building creaked slowly back and forth, but the words on it were clear enough — INN OF THE WHISPERING GHOST.

There were hitching posts for horses in front of the stores. But no horses neighed. No voices came from any of the shops. No one walked on the street.

"It's so quiet here I can hear my heart beating," Jo-Beth said softly.

A small breeze scattered red dust along the wooden walks. Large round spiky objects came rolling toward them, whipped along by the wind.

"They're weird," Mary Rose said, moving out of the way. "What are they anyway?"

"That's just tumbleweed." Mr. Onetree looked down at Jo-Beth and rumpled her hair. "Sometimes it's called witch grass."

"*Witch* grass?" Jo-Beth shuddered. She stared at the tumbleweeds and wondered how a witch could ride on anything that spiky. And since it rolled and rolled, how did a witch stay on?

"I don't like it here," Mary Rose said. "This is just a going-nowhere street."

Jo-Beth looked interested. "What's a going-nowhere street?"

"It's a street that has no place to go. It doesn't take you anywhere. It just stops all of a sudden. It doesn't make any sense at all!"

Just then a piece of paper blew along the street and wrapped itself around Jo-Beth's legs. Jo-Beth stood absolutely still. "Take it off," she begged, afraid to look down and see what it was.

Mary Rose pulled it free. "It's some kind of old poster." She held it out so they could all read it.

WANTED
DEAD OR ALIVE.
One hundred dollars for the
capture of Sorehead Jones for the
Dastardly Murder of Dirty Pete

3

Coming to Get You!

"Is this more atmosphere?" Jo-Beth asked. She didn't like it one bit. Atmosphere was better when she was sitting comfortably in her own house watching TV, with Mary Rose beside her and her mother getting Harry Two ready for bed. "What's wrong with this place? Why isn't anybody here? Is everybody dead or something?"

"In a way," her father replied thoughtfully. "I think we've found ourselves a ghost town."

"I know about ghost towns," Mary Rose said promptly. "They're places where people used to live and then went away. Miners. They just got up and left everything behind and never came back. So then the towns died." She gazed at the street and the stores. "It's awfully sad."

"I've had enough, Daddy. We can go now." Jo-Beth started to walk back to the car.

"In a minute. There's nothing to be afraid of, Jo-Beth," he added. "There's nobody around here but us . . ."

"And Sorehead Jones." She pointed at the poster.

"That happened long, long ago. Just be patient. I've never been to a ghost town before. I can't leave without looking around a little bit." Even as he was talking, Mr. Onetree began to cross the street.

"Do you want to wait in the car with me?" Jo-Beth begged her sister.

"What for? I've never been in a place like this either. You can stay here if you want to but I'm going with Daddy."

Jo-Beth ran after her sister. She wasn't going to be left behind, to stand alone on this going-nowhere street. As she caught up to them, Jo-Beth drew a deep breath, ready to insist that they leave right away.

Mr. Onetree was studying a scale in the window of a store marked ASSAY OFFICE. Before she could speak, he pointed to some pans near the scale. "Look at that. Gold pans. And that scale was for weighing gold dust. Imagine the miners coming in with their little sacks of ore. The story of this town is right here, in this place. A gold strike that ran out. A town born, and a town left to die." His face became thoughtful. "Wouldn't it be great to stay here for a few days and pan for gold in one of the streams? Just to see if there was any left? Just to get some idea of what those miners must have felt?"

Mr. Onetree had a faraway look in his eye, the same kind of look that Jo-Beth got when she began daydreaming.

Mary Rose wanted to tell him that the best thing they could do was get into the car and go find a motel, a real motel, but she held back. What good would it do? Once her father got into this kind of mood, he couldn't seem to think of anything but what he wanted to do. Her mother would have said right now, "Harry, let's be practical. The children are hungry, and getting tired. We can always come back if you still want to. Later."

"But," Mary Rose thought, "if I tell him that, he'll think I'm spoiling his fun."

"I'm going to take a look in the saloon. And then the livery stable . . ."

"You're taking your life in your hands," Jo-Beth warned. She had heard that on a TV program once. She had never dreamed that she would ever be able to say something that dramatic herself. Jo-Beth liked the feel of the words so much she repeated them in a deep voice.

Mr. Onetree grinned and went on. "And there is no way I'm going to miss taking a look at the Inn. You girls can either wait for me in the car or go see anything that appeals to you."

With that, Mr. Onetree went striding off

before Jo-Beth could make any other objection.

"I suppose we might as well look around," Mary Rose commented. "I think I'm going over there." She pointed to the PALACE DANCE HALL AND OPERA HOUSE.

Like her father, Mary Rose moved away quickly, running across the street toward the dance hall.

"Wait! Mary Rose. Wait for me!" Sit in the car, all by herself, in the middle of a ghost town? Not Jo-Beth!

The breeze had grown stronger. Tumbleweeds were heading straight for her — no, not tumbleweeds. Witch grass.

Jo-Beth could feel the small fine hairs on her arm beginning to stand up, and she was getting that prickly cold feeling in her spine. She didn't need anyone to tell her; she *knew* something was here, and she wasn't about to wait for it to come and get her.

"Look at this," Mary Rose cried when the two girls entered the building. Chairs were leaning against tables; some were lying on their sides on the floor. Bottles with faded labels, some with small glasses beside them, were on a long wooden bar.

"This isn't an opera house." Mary Rose had been to the opera once. She hadn't liked the music, but she had enjoyed the dancing and the colorful costumes. "But there *is* a stage. I guess maybe they had singing and dancing here long ago. Come on. I want to go up closer."

Jo-Beth turned so that she was facing backwards. "This way," she explained, "I can see what's behind us while you can see what's in front of us."

"You're so silly," Mary Rose began, then stopped and gasped.

"What is it? What's the matter?" Jo-Beth asked. She wanted to close her eyes so she wouldn't see whatever it was that had made Mary Rose catch her breath, but she didn't dare in case someone — something — might be creeping up unexpectedly.

"That curtain. It moved," Mary Rose whispered. She peered at the faded red draperies that hung on each side of the small stage. After a moment, she shrugged. "It must have been the wind whistling in through the cracks."

Jo-Beth put a hand over her chest. "I think I'm having a heart attack."

"Seven-year-old girls don't have heart attacks."

"Seven-and-a-*half*!"

"Seven-and-a-half-year-olds don't, either."

Jo-Beth moved closer to her sister. "Mary Rose, I swear I'm not pretending now. I feel *eyes* looking at me."

"Don't do that, Jo-Beth," Mary Rose said fiercely. "Now you've got me feeling all creepy . . ."

At that moment, the building was flooded with the sound of a man singing. It was like nothing the girls had ever heard, a strange scratchy voice, high and loud, saying words they couldn't understand.

Jo-Beth froze. Her feet seemed to grow roots right through the hard wooden floor. Mary Rose grabbed her sister's hand and pulled her along. As they ran out of the building, the man's voice chased after them. Jo-Beth didn't have to understand the queer words; she knew that he was telling them, *Coming-to-get-you! Coming-to-get-you!*

The girls ran smack into their father, who was just about to enter.

"Ghosts," Jo-Beth babbled.

Mr. Onetree listened. "Nonsense," he said at once. "Can't you tell that's just an old record? Come on. Let's see where the music is coming from."

"I'll never go back in there, not in a million years," Jo-Beth insisted, but in a moment she found herself following her father and sister back inside.

"It's coming from backstage." Mr. Onetree jumped up onto the stage and disappeared behind the curtain.

When Mary Rose and Jo-Beth found him, he was staring down at an old phonograph. It was in a dark wooden cabinet, which had a handle at the side. A needle was wobbling its way across a record that was spinning round and round. The voice, which had a harsh tinny sound up close, was coming from a large horn that served as a speaker.

"What do you know?" Mr. Onetree said with interest. "It's a Victrola. An old-fashioned wind-up Victrola."

Jo-Beth hunched her shoulders. The silence, now that her father had reached over and stopped the music, was louder than ever.

"Imagine letting a Victrola scare us," Mary Rose said, sounding annoyed.

"The Victrola doesn't scare me," Jo-Beth said in a trembling voice. "All I want to know is, if this is a ghost town and there's nobody here but us, *who put the record on?*"

4

"Our Fate Is Sealed"

"I think we ought to get out of here," Mary Rose said firmly.

"Fine," her father said at once. "We'll go over to the Inn and investigate . . . "

Jo-Beth didn't wait to hear what it was her father wanted to investigate. "Daddy. Mary Rose doesn't mean that we should just get out of this *building*. She means we should get out of this whole town." She waved her arms around so that her father could understand exactly what she hoped they would do. "Please. Even if we have to drive forever."

Mary Rose turned to her father. "I think it's a good idea, us getting out of here right away. Somebody sure doesn't want us to hang around."

"Or some*thing*," Jo-Beth added hollowly.

"You girls aren't serious. You expect a newspaperman to walk away . . ."

"Yes," said Mary Rose.

Jo-Beth nodded her head as hard as she could.

"I'll tell you what. You girls wait in the car while I . . . "

"No," Mary Rose said.

"No," said Jo-Beth.

They had been walking as they talked, with Jo-Beth facing forward this time since her father was right beside her. Suddenly Jo-Beth stopped walking. Her body went stiff as a board. Slowly she pointed a shaking finger.

Mr. Onetree followed the direction of her finger and saw nothing frightening.

"What is it now?" he asked.

Jo-Beth could hardly get the words out. "The car. It's gone."

"Gone? What do you mean, gone? That's impossible."

The impossible, however, had happened.

The car was most certainly missing.

Mr. Onetree raced along the street. He reached the spot where he had parked the car, then put his hands on his hips and shook his head. When the girls caught up with him, they understood why he was shaking his head.

The car was not missing after all. It had rolled down the hill and had landed in a ditch beside the dirt road.

Mr. Onetree smacked his forehead with the palm of his hand. "The emergency brake! I forgot to use it."

"I knew it," Mary Rose cried. "I just knew this would happen."

Because Mr. Onetree was feeling guilty, he snapped, "Mary Rose, do you have to be so right all the time?"

Mary Rose looked down at the road and started to move the dirt around with the point of her shoe. "I'm not going to cry," she told herself. "I'm not!"

Meanwhile Jo-Beth was nodding her head up and down like a puppet on a string. "We're doomed. Trapped in a dead town with a whispering ghost."

"What whispering ghost?" Mary Rose muttered crossly. "The only whispering ghost is on that dumb old sign."

But it was too good a word to drop, so Jo-Beth repeated it, "Doomed," stretching it out as far as she could.

"Let's not get carried away, Jo-Beth. There's nothing I can do about the car right now. I'll have to figure some way to get it up out of the ditch. Meanwhile, we're stuck here for the night . . ."

The girls groaned at their father's words. Stay here? Overnight? In this place?

" . . . so we might as well make the best of it," he continued. "There are a couple of flashlights in the trunk I think I can get at." He made his way carefully down into the ditch.

Mary Rose watched his every move, but Jo-Beth kept looking across the way at the Inn. She felt as if eyes were staring at them. No.

She *knew* eyes were fixed on them. But maybe if they all got into the car and locked the door. . . . When she asked her father, however, he explained, very reasonably, that it would be too uncomfortable.

"I'm sure we can find someplace in the Inn to stretch out for the night."

"This is it," Jo-Beth said as they stepped up on the wooden walk. "Our fate is sealed!"

"We can't stay here, Daddy," Mary Rose exclaimed when they entered the Inn. She had decided the only way to act now was to pretend that he hadn't hurt her feelings. "Just look at this place."

The walls, which had once been covered with fine red cloth, were ragged and peeling in spots. Two easy chairs, sagging in the middle, were covered with dust.

Jo-Beth wrinkled her nose. "What's that funny smell?"

Her father answered, "That's the musty smell places get when they've been closed in

and shut up for a long time."

Mary Rose wandered to a rocker placed near the front window. She sat down and almost immediately jumped up again. "Daddy. This seat is warm."

"I knew it," Jo-Beth cried, and told them about her feeling that eyes had been watching them all this while.

"So there really is a ghost," Mary Rose said, shocked at the idea.

"Ghosts don't warm the seats of rockers."
Mr. Onetree was very firm about that. "Someone is playing tricks on us, and I am going to
search this place from top to bottom until I
find the person who's doing it."

"Couldn't we just go and lock ourselves in
the car until morning? Jo-Beth begged.

Her father was turning his head, first one
way, then another. "I smell coffee." Sniffing,
he started to walk past the stairway toward
the back of the hotel. He tracked the smell of
the coffee to the kitchen, and stopped in the
doorway. The girls stopped, too.

On the kitchen table, steam curled from
the spout of an old coffee pot. In a large black
crusty pan beans were bubbling. The girls
had never seen a stove like this one — a black
coal stove that had a round pipe chimney
going up to the ceiling.

A loaf of bread was half cut; a sharp knife
in the loaf appeared to have been placed
there only a moment ago.

A newspaper was folded as if someone had been reading it.

But no one was there!

"Now I guess we'll go back to the car," Jo-Beth said promptly.

"We don't mind being uncomfortable. We like being uncomfortable," Mary Rose agreed.

Mr. Onetree just sat down at the kitchen table without answering. He pursed his lips, as if he were whistling, but he didn't make a sound. His eyes were quite thoughtful.

The two girls exchanged glances. They knew that look very well. It meant that Mr. Onetree was working on an idea for his newspaper column.

Jo-Beth regarded her father solemnly. So a will-o'-the-wisp wasn't a leprechaun or a Martian, she thought. A will-o'-the-wisp was a ghost, and that was what he wanted to chase. She closed her eyes and wished as hard as she could. She wished that this was one will-o'-the-wisp that her father would never catch!

5

Beware the
Odd-Numbered Doors

"Well," Mr. Onetree said later, smacking his lips. "Our friend the ghost did us a big favor. I was hungry."

"Mmmmm." Mary Rose was just finishing the last bite of her bean sandwich. "So was I."

"I never had a ghost sandwich before." Jo-Beth wiped her mouth with the back of her hand. She felt much better, now that her stomach was full.

Mr. Onetree handed one of the flashlights to Mary Rose. "We'll need both lights to find our way upstairs."

"What about me?" Jo-Beth asked.

"You take the paper. Roll it up," her father

said with a grin, "and if the ghost shows up, hit him over the head with it."

Jo-Beth giggled. She could see herself hitting the ghost over the head, and the ghost begging her to stop.

Mary Rose looked at her father. Tears began to sting her eyes. Why couldn't he have said something silly like that to her? Why didn't he like her anymore? Was it because Jo-Beth was younger? And maybe more exciting to be with? Well, he wasn't any better than Jo-Beth, joking when they were trapped in such an awful place.

Her fingers tightened on the flashlight. It was scary here. Mary Rose didn't know which might be worse — trying to find their way back to the car along the dark street, or spending the night in this strange place.

"All right, girls. This is it." Mr. Onetree led them back to the lobby and the steps going to the second floor. Even two flashlights didn't push back the darkness. In some way, they made it even eerier.

"We'll all get some sleep, wake up fresh in the morning, and then lay this ghost to rest," he went on.

"Lay the ghost to rest? You mean we're going to bury him?" Jo-Beth asked in panic.

"That's just an expression." Mary Rose didn't like this kind of talk any better than her sister did. But at least she understood it. Being ten and a half going on eleven was a big help at times. "Daddy just means that tomorrow he'll find out what's going on, that's all."

As they made their way upstairs, Jo-Beth stared hard at the wall. Ghosts could walk through anything — walls, closed doors, anything. They moaned and clanked chains. They beckoned, motioning with long bony fingers. And the air around them was always cold, very, very cold.

She shivered.

Wasn't the temperature dropping?

What was that sound? Was it a whisper? If

she turned around, quickly, would *it* be there behind her?

She half-lifted her rolled up newspaper.

There was a hallway at the top of the stairway. A row of doors on each side of the hall had numbers on them. The even-numbered doors were just to the right of the stairway.

Mr. Onetree opened the door closest to him and, flashing the light around inside, finally spoke. "This looks all right."

It was a small room with a single bed pushed against one wall. On the other side was a roughly painted dresser. On top of the dresser there was a big white china bowl, a pitcher, a soap dish without soap, and a rag that might once have been a towel. On the floor beside the dresser was a chamber pot.

"What's that?" Jo-Beth asked, which was not surprising, for she had never seen a chamber pot before.

Mr. Onetree started to explain. "They didn't have bathrooms indoors in the old

days. They had outhouses, and for conven-
ience, chamber pots."

"You mean there isn't even a bathroom!"
Jo-Beth declared.

"Please. Spare me. Take this room or the
one next door, but let's get some sleep. And
there's nothing to worry about. See? There's
a lock on the door."

Mary Rose examined the lock. In it was a
big old-fashioned iron key.

"If you need me, just bang on the wall. Or
yell. Whatever." Mr. Onetree was so tired his
eyes were beginning to close while he was still
standing.

Mary Rose pushed her sister out of the
door and into the next room.

"We don't have our toothbrushes or paja-
mas or anything," Jo-Beth grumbled.

Mary Rose yawned. "Just sleep in your un-
derwear. Get into bed. I'll be back in a
minute."

Jo-Beth, who had just seated herself gin-
gerly on the edge of the bed, leaped to her

feet. "Where are you going? Don't leave me here alone. Suppose somebody comes after me while you're gone."

"I'm just going into another room to use the chamber pot. If anything happens, just bang on the wall, like Daddy said."

"Can't you use it here? I'll turn around, Mary Rose."

"No. I happen to like my privacy."

"Privacy? At a time like this? You're not going to take the flashlight? I'll be all alone here in the dark."

Mary Rose had certainly planned to take the light with her.

"I'm coming right back," she explained.

"I won't stay in the dark. I'll come with you." Even at home, Jo-Beth always had a light on, all night, in her room.

Usually Mary Rose understood. But this had been a most upsetting day.

"Oh, keep your old light," she snapped, and marched out of the room, so angry she forgot to be afraid of anything at all.

Jo-Beth locked the door and got into bed. Then she got out of bed and unlocked the door. It would be terrible if Mary Rose couldn't get back into the room in a hurry.

Just as Jo-Beth turned the key in the lock, Mary Rose screamed, a long, terrified wail that ended as suddenly as it began.

Jo-Beth whipped the door open and saw her father at his door, flashlight in hand.

"Was that Mary Rose? What's happened? Where is she?"

"She went to get privacy," Jo-Beth sobbed. Something terrible must have happened. Suppose she never saw Mary Rose again? Why couldn't she have been nicer to her sister? She really did love Mary Rose, even though she had tried to take the flashlight away.

Both Mr. Onetree and Jo-Beth noticed the slightly open door across the hall at the same time. Jo-Beth started to run across, but Mr. Onetree caught her and pushed her back.

"Stand away, Jo-Beth," he commanded.

Carefully he began to push the door open wider. He felt a gust of wind and leaped back.

There was no room behind the door, only open space.

"Mary Rose. Mary Rose," he shouted into the air.

For what seemed like a long time, there was no answer. Then came a voice, crying weakly.

Mr. Onetree flashed his light around and then down. Jo-Beth, holding on to him as hard as she could, looked down, too.

A wagon loaded with hay was just under the room from which Mary Rose had stepped out into nothingness. Mary Rose was lying on the hay.

"Stay there," Mr. Onetree shouted. "I'm coming right down."

He raced downstairs, with Jo-Beth running as fast as she could. "Please," she prayed, "don't let her be dead and I'll never argue with her again."

By the time they reached her, Mary Rose was climbing down from the hay wagon,

brushing small broken pieces of straw from her hair and clothing.

"Are you all right?" her father demanded.

"I just had the breath knocked out of me. What kind of a room has a door and no room behind it?" She sounded more angry than hurt.

Jo-Beth was so glad Mary Rose was safe that she began to scold her sister. "You and your privacy. You scared us half to death."

"I scared you? I wasn't exactly laughing all the way down. Honestly!"

"Let's go on back to our rooms. And this time, both of you stay put!" he said angrily.

"I wasn't the one . . ."

"Never mind, Jo-Beth." Mr. Onetree didn't want to hear any explanations.

When they were back upstairs, Jo-Beth asked quietly, because she thought her father was still angry, "Do you think all the rooms are like the one Mary Rose went through? I mean the rooms with the odd numbers on them?"

Mr. Onetree was sorry he had shouted at his daughters. He knew he had done so only because he had been so worried.

"Let's take a look and see." One by one, he opened the doors to the odd-numbered rooms across the hall, making the girls stand back. All the doors opened into space.

"Something weird is going on around here," Jo-Beth said with dark satisfaction.

"She's right. This place is spooky," Mary Rose agreed.

"Too bad somebody didn't put a sign up in the hall — beware the odd-numbered doors," Mr. Onetree added.

Beware the odd-numbered doors! The words danced in Jo-Beth's mind. How was she expected to go to sleep after this?

"Daddy. Stay with us for a little while. Just till we get sleepy," she begged. "I wish you had a book to read to us." That was always so nice, settling back in bed, listening to a story until her eyes began to close.

"I don't have anything to read . . . "

"The paper," Mary Rose remembered. "You can read to us from that old newspaper." She picked up the paper from the dresser, unrolled it, and pointed to one of the columns. "Read that, Daddy." She climbed into bed and snuggled close to her sister.

"This story is called 'The Legend of the Whispering Ghost.' That's not exactly a bedtime story. Are you sure that's what you want?"

Mary Rose nodded. Jo-Beth sat up. She hugged her knees and regarded her father with shivering delight.

The Legend of the Whispering Ghost. At last she would find out if there really was a ghost in this weird place.

6

The Legend of
the Whispering Ghost

"This is an old newspaper," Mr. Onetree said. "It's dated 1905." He read to himself for a moment before going on. "It says here that this used to be called the Grand Hotel."

"Grand? This old place?" Jo-Beth wrinkled her nose. "It isn't even finished. How can a place be grand if it has doors and no rooms?"

"Never mind all that." Mary Rose wanted her father to get on with the reading.

Mr. Onetree had placed the flashlights on the dresser and was holding the paper near them so he could see the print. The light threw his shadow up on the wall and a little way across the ceiling. The shadow flickered back and forth as he moved his head.

Jo-Beth was sure she could hear a coyote howling its lonesome call off in the distance. Weren't there slow dragging footsteps in the hall? Was the doorknob turning, quietly, secretly?

She was so wonderfully frightened she could hardly breathe.

Mr. Onetree began to read.

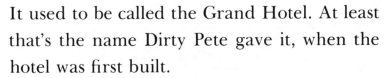

It used to be called the Grand Hotel. At least that's the name Dirty Pete gave it, when the hotel was first built.

Dirty Pete started out as a drifter, going from one mining town to another, always hoping to make that one lucky strike. He was a rough man, and a tough man, and a stubborn man as well. He was a short, square man, who looked as if he had spent his life rolling in the mud.

Dirty Pete was the first man to find his way

DIRTY PETE

50

to Skull Valley Hill. That was what he called it when he found two skulls at the foot of the small mountain. The skulls glittered and glared at Dirty Pete, because someone had put gold ore where their eyes had once been. But that didn't scare Dirty Pete away.

He'd found his gold.

No one knows how the word got around. It wasn't long before other miners came to Skull Valley. Little by little the stores went up.

Dirty Pete wanted his town to be fancier than all the other mining towns he'd seen. He used some of his gold to build the Grand Hotel. And then, just to show the world how rich he was, he built the Palace Dance Hall and Opera House.

A lot went on in Skull Valley. There was music for those who wanted it, high-class music Dirty Pete called it. He couldn't get real singers to come to the Opera House, so he bought a Victrola and played records. Dirty Pete never let anybody else touch those records. He put them on himself.

There was a different kind of music over at the saloon, and a lot of whooping-it-up there, too.

And there was the sound of gunfire as well. It wasn't long before Skull Valley had its own cemetery along with its opera house and its beautiful hotel.

One day there was a new face in town. It belonged to Sorehead Jones, a man with silver hair and blue eyes that burned like the sky on fire. A scar like forked lightning ran down one side of his face, from his eyebrow to his chin. No one dared ask how he got that strange scar.

Sorehead Jones wanted gold, but he didn't want to dig for it. He'd heard tell that Dirty Pete kept his gold hidden in a treasure chest.

Dirty Pete just laughed. Nobody would ever find his gold. Not Sorehead Jones. Not any other man in town.

Sorehead Jones stuck closer to Dirty Pete than his shadow. The more Dirty Pete laughed, the colder the look on Sorehead Jones's face became.

One day Sorehead forced a showdown. He came roaring into the hotel, waving his gun, and caught Dirty Pete as he was coming down the steps.

"Where is the gold?" Sorehead asked in a terrible whisper.

Dirty Pete stood looking at Jones with a sneering smile on his face. "You'll never find it."

"I'll ask you one last time."

Sorehead held his gun aimed straight and true, but Dirty Pete shot Sorehead just as the other man pulled the trigger.

"He's killed me," Dirty Pete cried, and fell dead.

Sorehead Jones disappeared somehow, leaving a trail of blood across the lobby of the Grand Hotel.

The sheriff tacked up WANTED posters all over town.

They found Sorehead ten days later, hiding out backstage at the Dance Hall. A record was playing on the Victrola.

Sorehead was still alive, just barely breathing. "Dirty Pete put the record on," he babbled.

"Dirty Pete's dead," someone objected.

"I tell you he put the record on, still sneering at me," Sorehead gasped. "He's still protecting his gold. Well, you can bury me wide and bury me deep. But he hasn't got the best of me yet. I'll haunt this place till I find it."

They put a heavy stone on Sorehead's grave. But visitors at the Grand Hotel swore they could hear Sorehead's dragging footsteps in the hall and on the stairs. They claimed they could hear his ghost whispering, "Where is the gold? Where is the gold?"

After a while, someone took down the old sign and put the new one up — The Inn of the Whispering Ghost.

No one has ever found Dirty Pete's gold.

No one has ever bothered to take down the WANTED posters.

The town is dying.

But the Legend of the Whispering Ghost lives on.

<hr/>

"Wow! What a really neat story." Mary Rose rubbed at the goose bumps on her arms.

Mr. Onetree was frowning. "It seems to me I've heard this before. Or something like it."

"You mean it's all true?" Jo-Beth asked.

"I mean that I have a funny feeling about this story, but I can't put my finger on it."

Mary Rose yawned. "You sound awfully mysterious yourself, Daddy."

"Bedtime. Here, Jo-Beth. You can hold on to the flashlight."

After their father left the room, Jo-Beth lay back and stared up at the ceiling. Then she turned around and glared at her sister. How could Mary Rose fall asleep so quickly and so deeply at a time like this?

"That girl doesn't have a nerve in her body," she said out loud, hoping her voice would wake Mary Rose. That's what their Aunt Madge said about her husband: "That man doesn't have a nerve in his body."

The silence pressed against Jo-Beth's ears. It wasn't a friendly quiet; it had a waiting kind of feel to it, as if something was on the edge of happening. And then a faint sound made Jo-Beth listen hard. There! She heard it again. It was the slow clip-clopping of a horse's hoofs, steady, coming closer and closer.

Jo-Beth wanted to dive under the covers, but curiosity drove her to the window. At first she could see nothing, only the going-no-where street waiting, just as she was waiting. And then rider and horse came into view. The man was dressed all in black, a dreadful shadow in the moonlight.

"Make him go away," she prayed. "Don't let

him stop." But the horseman did stop, directly under the window. His pale hair glinted moon-silver. When he raised his head and stared up at Jo-Beth, his eyes were deep burning holes. Along one side of his face there ran a long cruel scar.

"Sorehead Jones!" Jo-Beth moaned. Yet she couldn't turn her eyes away.

His whisper pierced the silent night.

"Where is the gold?"

7

"So You've Come Back, Black Bart"

Someone was shaking Jo-Beth, shaking her hard. Jo-Beth's eyes flew open with alarm. Had Sorehead Jones come back? Was he here, in the room?

"Oh. It's you," she said crossly to her sister. With the sun shining brightly through the window, it was hard to believe that she had actually seen the ghost last night. Maybe she had only dreamed it all. She sat up and frowned. "Waking me up like that. You just took ten years off my life, do you know that, Mary Rose?"

"I wish you'd stop repeating everything you hear," Mary Rose scolded. "Do you ever listen to yourself? Ten years off your life. You're only seven . . ."

" . . . and a half." She liked the way she talked. Some day she would act on the stage. Then she could be dramatic all the time if she felt like it. "Where's Daddy? Is he still sleeping?"

"He's downstairs poking around. I heard him go down."

"How do you know it was Daddy? Maybe it was Sorehead Jones."

Mary Rose frowned. Was Jo-Beth going to start all over again? "Ghosts don't poke . . ."

"How do you know what ghosts do?" Jo-Beth flared. "You've never even seen a ghost." It was on the tip of her tongue to tell her sister what she had seen from the window. Then she changed her mind. What good would it do? Mary Rose wouldn't believe her. Her father would only laugh. Only this time it hadn't been imagination. She felt sure now that she had seen the ghost.

"I'm going down."

"Wait. Please wait, Mary Rose. I won't be dramatic anymore. I promise. I don't want to stay up here alone. Just wait till I get my clothes on." Jo-Beth dressed quickly, in case her sister decided to go down without her.

Together, the two girls ran down the steps.

Their father was standing just outside the entrance. "I have an idea about this place," he told them when they rushed to greet him. "I don't know why I didn't think of it last night. I guess it was because I was so tired. Come along."

"What kind of idea?"

"Where are we going?"

Mr. Onetree didn't bother to reply. He just began to walk quickly toward the nearest store, where he tried to turn the knob on the door.

"Why are we going into the hat store?" Jo-Beth wondered.

"Millinery," Mary Rose corrected, reading the sign. "'Madam Margo's Millinery.'"

"Isn't the door locked?" Jo-Beth asked her

father, paying no attention to her sister. "Big show-off," Jo-Beth thought. "Just because she can read practically anything."

Mr. Onetree shook his head. "It isn't locked. Just jammed tight." He put his weight against the door and pushed. The door creaked and moved just a little. Mr. Onetree pushed harder. This time the door swung open.

"Step in, ladies," Mr. Onetree said, bowing. "And step right out again."

Jo-Beth giggled and went through the doorway. "Hey!"

Mary Rose followed, and blinked in surprise. "Where's the store?" she cried. "There's nothing here. We're just outside again."

"Are all the buildings like this, Daddy? Are they all just make-believe?"

"Mostly. I got up early and investigated. They all have false fronts, except for just a few places, like the Opera House, and the feed store, and maybe a few other places I haven't looked into yet. And of course the Inn."

"The Inn isn't real either," Mary Rose said. "I know. I stepped into a room that wasn't there."

"This sure is a peculiar ghost town," Jo-Beth pronounced. "Is that the way people used to build things in the olden days?"

"It's not any kind of a ghost town, as far as I can tell. It was probably a movie set for some Western picture."

"But Daddy, what about that newspaper we found? What about Dirty Pete and Sorehead Jones?" Mary Rose wanted to know.

"I don't think they're any more real than anything else around here."

"No, Daddy. You're wrong," Jo-Beth blurted. "Sorehead Jones is real. I saw him with my own eyes. Last night. When everybody else was sleeping," she added, shivering.

"Oh, honestly," Mary Rose said. "If this is a movie set," she went on, ignoring Jo-Beth, "where are the people?"

"Not here. This place must have been abandoned a long time ago, from the looks of things. But never mind that. I have a surprise for you."

"You found food. We're going to have breakfast," Jo-Beth said promptly. "I'm starved."

"That's not it, is it, Daddy?" Mary Rose was studying her father's face. "It's a real surprise, right? A nice one. I can tell."

"I took a walk up the hill, and when I got around to the other side, what do you think I saw?"

"A helicopter," Jo-Beth guessed wildly.

"Why would a helicopter land here in the middle of nowhere? Come on, Daddy. I don't want to play guessing games. What did you see?" Mary Rose asked.

"A town. Houses. Cars. And even a couple of people."

"We're saved. We're saved." Jo-Beth hugged her father.

"How are we going to get there?" Mary Rose wondered. "We can't drive."

"We'll walk. It can't be more than a couple of miles or so."

Mary Rose looked up at the sky. The sun was already making the day quite warm.

"If we're going to take a hike," she said, "I want to change into shorts. We'll be too hot in our jeans."

"Good idea," Mr. Onetree told her. "Come on. I'll walk you back to the car."

Mary Rose looked all around. "You don't have to, Daddy. I don't see anybody. Just give me the car key."

"Wait a minute," Jo-Beth protested. "I think Daddy should come with us."

"Jo-Beth." Mary Rose almost hissed. "If you don't mind, I would like some privacy."

"What for?" Jo-Beth was surprised.

"Girls. Can we get this show on the road?" Mr. Onetree was impatient. He handed the car key to his older daughter. "It isn't much of a ditch and you won't have any trouble getting into the car. Just be careful. And listen," he added, "there's a bag of jellybeans in the glove compartment. Bring them along and we can eat them on our way to town."

Jo-Beth beamed. No one had ever let her eat jellybeans for breakfast before. "Beat you to the car, Mary Rose."

"Bet you don't!"

The two girls began to race as fast as they could down the street.

Mr. Onetree watched them, smiling. And then the smile disappeared.

Something cold and hard was pressing against the back of his head.

A voice spoke. It had the sound of an iron chain being pulled over gravel.

"So," the voice said. "So you've come back, Black Bart."

8

Meet Sourdough Sam

Mr. Onetree started to turn his head. "Wait a minute . . ."

"Don't make me pull this trigger. I'm itching to pull it. If I wasn't a lawman, I would pull it."

Mr. Onetree stood very, very still. His lips felt dry. "If I could turn around and talk to you," he managed to say, trying not to move a muscle.

"You can't smooth talk your way out of this. Put your hands on top of your head."

Mr. Onetree did exactly as he was told.

"Now march."

"Where are you taking me?"

"To the jail. The boys want to put a rope around your neck here and now. But they've got me to reckon with. You're going to jail, Black Bart. You're going to get a fair trial, and then we'll hang you."

"If you'd take a look at me," Mr. Onetree said desperately, "you'd see I'm not the man you're looking for. My name is Harry Onetree . . ."

"You claiming to be an Indian? You take me for some kind of fool? Black Bart you were, and Black Bart you are. And Black Bart is what we'll put on your tombstone."

Mr. Onetree decided the only thing he could do was walk toward the jail. Maybe it, too, was a false-front building. If so, then he could walk in and race out the other side. Or maybe he could wrestle the gun away from the other man somehow.

They had reached the jailhouse. Mr. One-tree's heart sank. Like the opera house and the hotel, it seemed to be solid enough. He walked across the rough wooden floor, the gun still at his neck, through a door at the back of the room.

"I'm locking you up, Black Bart. I'll send Tillie around in a while with some grub for you. Not that you deserve to be fed."

Once inside the cell, Mr. Onetree was able to turn around at last.

"That's right. Study me good and hard. You finally met your match in this lawman." The man tapped the silver star on his leather vest.

Mr. Onetree paid no attention to the key turning in the lock. He was too busy staring at the man who had captured him.

The sheriff stood tall and lean and keen-eyed. His hands rested easily near the silver-handled guns in his gun belt, not touching the guns but ready for a lightning-quick draw if necessary. He held his head high and proud, and when he spoke his voice was firm and strong. You could tell this sheriff kept his town in good order.

The more Mr. Onetree stared, the more

puzzled he became. There was something about the sheriff, something about the way he moved, the sound of his voice . . .

"Don't I know you from someplace?" Mr. Onetree asked, thinking hard.

"Don't he know me from someplace!" The sheriff chuckled. "You hear that, Jud?" he called over his shoulder.

Mr. Onetree tried to catch a glimpse of the man called Jud. But no one was there.

"Who's Jud? Can I talk to him?" Mr. Onetree asked.

"Hey, Jud. Here's Black Bart behind bars, asking who's Jud. Ain't that rich? Ain't that a knee-grabber?" He listened for an answer, and then nodded his head as if someone had spoken. But Mr. Onetree heard nothing.

"I tell you I know your voice." Mr. Onetree ran his hand through his hair. "If I could only put a name to it . . ."

The sheriff lounged against the wall, looking amused. "You are a caution, Bart. I'll give you that." He straightened up suddenly, came

71

closer to the cell. His eyes were frosty. "We've had a clean town since you rode out, and I aim to keep it that way."

Those watchful eyes that seemed to see deep inside of you. That hard line around the lips. Those long fingers tossing the keys up and down, so out of reach and yet so close . . .

Close up. A close-up. That's what they call it in the movies when the camera moves in and shows you just the face, or the hands. Close-ups. Cameras.

Something clicked in Mr. Onetree's mind.

"You're an actor. At least you used to be. I saw you in a lot of Westerns when I was a kid. You had a funny name . . . I'll remember it. It'll come to me . . . Sourdough! Sourdough Sam!" Mr. Onetree was so relieved he began to laugh. "You were terrific. You were one of my favorites . . ."

"You remember me?" The other man smiled, a big smile that warmed his eyes and moved the wrinkles around on his face.

"You've changed some," Mr. Onetree admitted. "But that voice and those eyes are the same. It's all coming back. I saw you in so many movies. *The Dastardly Murder of Dirty Pete*! I loved that one! No wonder the story seemed so familiar."

"That sure goes back a way," Sourdough Sam said. "So you were one of my fans."

"I used to save cards with your photograph on them." Mr. Onetree didn't mention that he hadn't looked at the cards since he was a small boy. "Good old Dirty Pete and Sorehead Jones! Wait till I tell the girls. You played the sheriff, just like you're doing now. And you put Black Bart in jail." Mr. Onetree shook his head. "So you were just putting on an act. You certainly convinced me, Sam. How about letting me out now?"

Sourdough Sam stiffened. The smile faded away. The frost came back into his eyes. The steel came back into his voice.

"Up to your old tricks, are you, Bart? Hey, Jud. Get in here!"

Mr. Onetree couldn't believe it. One minute the other man had been himself, Sourdough Sam. The next minute he was the character he had played on the screen. He really thought he was the sheriff.

Mr. Onetree felt desperate. "He's mad," Mr. Onetree thought. "He'll scare the girls. And I can't get out to warn them. Or help them." If only he could reason with Sam . . . Maybe if he went along with the play-acting . . .

"Sheriff," Mr. Onetree said, "I've got some unfinished business in town. Why don't you let me out for a little while, and then I'll come back. Word of honor. You know you can trust Black Bart."

"You always were quick with words, Bart. But it won't do you no good with me." Sam turned and listened to a voice that only he could hear. "Don't you worry none, Jud. I'm coming right back. I'll get rid of the boys out front. Ain't nobody going to spring Black Bart out of jail. Nobody!"

The sheriff left the room, with that special stride of his that Mr. Onetree had tried so hard to imitate when he was a little boy.

"Sam," Mr. Onetree called after him anxiously. "Wait. Listen . . ."

But Sourdough Sam was gone.

Mr. Onetree moved around his cell restlessly. He shook the iron bars, but they were solid. The walls were made of stone. The small window high on the back wall was barred, too.

Sam had taken the key to the cell with him. Suppose he forgot to come back? Suppose he forgot he was the sheriff!

Mr. Onetree suspected now that it was Sam who had frightened the girls by putting on the record in the dance hall. And it was Sam who had left his food on the table and disappeared when Mr. Onetree and the girls had gone to the Inn. What characters had he been play-acting then?

Maybe Sourdough Sam was harmless, just a man living in a fantasy world. But he could be dangerous.

Mr. Onetree rattled the bars. "Let me out," he shouted. At last he sank down on the cot at the back wall.

Who would Sam be when he met the girls? What would he say to them?

What would he do?

9

Looking for Curly

Jo-Beth and Mary Rose were halfway down the street when they saw Sourdough Sam coming toward them. Of course, they didn't know who he was, or what he had done to their father.

The girls had changed clothes and had come out of the car, eager to go find the town their father had seen. Surprised that he was nowhere in sight, they had begun shouting for him. Since Harry Onetree was in the jail at the other end of the town at the time, trying to get Sourdough Sam to let him out, he hadn't heard them calling.

"I wish Daddy wouldn't do things like this," Mary Rose said, between shouts.

"It's just because he's a newspaperman." Jo-Beth nodded her head wisely. "Newspaper men are always after a story."

"That's so silly. What kind of story could anybody find in this dumb old place?"

Jo-Beth didn't answer because she had just spied Sourdough Sam coming toward them. The soft black hat on his head was shabby and spotted with red dust. His shoulders were hunched inside a jacket much too large for him. Every once in a while he stopped walking and poked at the ground with the point of an unusual cane. As he came closer, the girls could see that the silver top of the cane was shaped like the head of a snake, jaws open, ready to strike. The snake's body curled down around and around the cane.

Jo-Beth was startled. "Who's he? Where did he come from?" She tried to pull her sister back as Mary Rose started to walk toward Sam. "We're not supposed to talk to strangers."

Mary Rose shook her arm free. "Maybe he's seen Daddy. Excuse me," she said politely when Sam stopped and looked at her. "Did you see a man around here? He's about five feet eleven and skinny . . . "

"He's our Daddy," Jo-Beth put in helpfully.

Sam peered at them over small spectacles that kept sliding down his nose. His eyes twinkled with good humor. "Why, it's Annabelle Faith and Charity Sue. You girls have growed so, I hardly recognized you. I expect you've just been to see the Widow Goodbody, maybe brought her some of your Ma's preserves. Wonderful woman, your Ma."

"We're not . . . " Mary Rose began, but Sam went right on talking.

"I swear, Charity Sue," he told Jo-Beth, "you look more like your Ma every day." He shook his head. "Prettiest schoolmarm that ever came to town, she was. Had every man jack of us eating out of her hand."

Jo-Beth's mouth opened in surprise. "Mommy? Why she never . . . What's the matter with you, Mary Rose? Why are you pinching me?"

"Don't answer him," her sister hissed. "Can't you tell there's something strange about him?"

"Shhh! He'll hear you."

Sam wasn't listening. He had turned away for a moment. "Howdy, Miz Platt. How've you been keeping?" he said to someone only he could see. He swept his hat from his head. "And Miz Tucker. Your boy still feeling poorly?"

Jo-Beth glanced all around. She felt the same way she had once when a spider had walked across her hand when she was at camp. She moved closer to Mary Rose. "Who's he talking to?" she asked in alarm.

"Nobody."

"Then let's go, Mary Rose. Please. Let's go!"

"Not till I find out where Daddy is. Please, sir. Have you seen our Daddy?" she asked as Sam turned back. "He has blond hair and blue eyes . . . "

"You don't have to tell old Doc about your Pa. Everybody in town knows Curly. I'm surprised at you, Annabelle Faith. You know your Pa is working the mine, same as he always does."

"Who's old Doc?" Jo-Beth asked, giving him a doubtful look.

Sourdough Sam put his hands on his hips and moved his head back and forth slowly. "I declare I don't know what's happened to good manners, standing there pretending you don't know me. Doc Peabody, who brought you into this world, Charity Sue. Didn't your Ma learn you no better than to tease your elders?"

"She didn't mean it, Dr. Peabody," Mary Rose put in quickly. She drew her eyebrows into a warning frown when Jo-Beth started to object. She half-turned and tapped her finger on the side of her forehead. Jo-Beth promptly moved behind her sister.

"Just call me Doc," Sam went on cheerfully. "Tell you what. It won't take me out of my way. I'll go along with you girls and see if we can't round up old Curly."

Mary Rose didn't know what to do. If her father had gone looking for "atmosphere," he could have decided to investigate the mine. Or maybe he had met old Doc, and old Doc had lured her father into the mine somehow. When that thought crossed Mary Rose's mind, she shuddered. Her heart skipped a beat. This was such a peculiar place, anything could have happened. Now she was convinced that her father needed help.

"Daddy's in the mine," she told Jo-Beth positively. "We have to go and get him."

"Are you sure you saw our Daddy go in there?" Jo-Beth asked Sam.

"Saw him plain as day. Now you girls walk on ahead of me." He began to swing his cane, just a little, but enough to make the girls move ahead quickly.

"I don't think Daddy's in the mine. Why would he go into the mine just when we're supposed to go find this town he saw?" Jo-Beth wanted to know.

"Daddy said he wouldn't mind staying here for a few days and looking for gold. Remember?"

"Is that another one of his will-o'-the-wisps?"

"I guess so." Mary Rose didn't want to frighten her sister by telling her what she really believed must have happened.

"I don't like old Doc Peabody," Jo-Beth muttered. She could hear the cane swishing behind them. "I don't think we should go into any old mine with him."

"You can stay outside if you want to. I'm going in." Mary Rose could be very stubborn when her mind was made up.

Jo-Beth, who had been feeling very uneasy, suddenly began to smile. They had reached a shack near the mine entrance. Standing quietly in front of it was a small gray donkey, one end of a long rope tied to a leather halter around its neck, the other end tied loosely to a post. Attached to the halter were several silver bells. As the girls approached the animal, the donkey bobbed its head up and down; the bells gave off a small tinkling sound.

"See? Amigo knows you," Sourdough Sam told them. "Now you girls wait here. I'm going into the shack to get some lanterns. Then we'll find Curly."

Jo-Beth told herself that this would be a good time to run away from the mine and from old Doc, but just then Amigo turned his head and looked at her.

"I'm going to give him some of the jellybeans," Jo-Beth said, opening the bag of candy.

"Donkeys don't eat jellybeans."

Jo-Beth had already put some of the beans in her hand and was holding them out to Amigo. The donkey's tongue felt warm and wet as it licked the candy from the palm of her hand.

"Try it," Jo-Beth urged her sister. "It tickles."

"You're dumb, Amigo. Do you know that?" Mary Rose asked as she too held out some beans.

Amigo just looked at Mary Rose with his big soft brown eyes.

"You feed old Amigo and you'll never get

rid of the critter," Sam warned as he came out of the shack carrying two lanterns. "Now Annabelle Faith," he said to Mary Rose, "you hold this light and you young 'uns stay real close. These tunnels go every which way. It's mighty easy to get lost down here."

"We'll watch you every minute," Mary Rose promised.

Sam went in through the mine entrance first. The two girls followed. Pulling the rope free from the post, Amigo ambled after them, his head nodding steadily, the bells tinkling, making a cheerful sound in the gloomy darkness.

Jo-Beth kept turning around to feed Amigo. In no time at all, the jellybeans were gone.

"That's it," Jo-Beth announced.

Amigo pushed Mary Rose, who stopped walking, turned, and pushed the donkey's head aside. "Stop that, you greedy little pig."

Jo-Beth laughed. "I didn't know you could

do magic. You just turned a donkey into a pig."

Mary Rose didn't speak. She stood absolutely still. Jo-Beth stopped, too. Even the donkey waited.

Somewhere in the distance there was the sound of water trickling. A cold wind swept through the tunnel.

"What's happening?" Jo-Beth cried.

Mary Rose's expression was grim. "It's Doc Peabody. He's gone."

Her announcement stunned Jo-Beth.

Why had he vanished?

What would happen to them now?

10

The Dancing Skeleton

"How could he just disappear like that?" Jo-Beth peered fearfully into the darkness. Mary Rose's lantern made the darkness worse, not better, changing the area outside her light into a deeper blackness.

"He must have sneaked off into another tunnel while we were busy with Amigo."

"I'm scared. This isn't just pretend, Mary Rose. I want to get out of here. I want Daddy," she wailed suddenly.

"That's what I want, too. Only I think that Doc Peabody has Daddy tied up in here some-place. I didn't tell you that before because then you wouldn't have come into the mine."

"You had no *right* to do that. Now what's going to happen to us?"

"No right? Who'll save Daddy if we don't?" Mary Rose flashed back. Because she was feeling guilty about having gotten them into trouble, she put into words something she had never said aloud before. "It's a fine way for you to act, anyway, considering that you're Daddy's favorite."

Jo-Beth's mouth opened in surprise. "Me?"

"That's right. You. Always joking around with you, and loving you on account of your imagination and all. He doesn't even like me very much. Oh, come on." Mary Rose brushed away her sudden tears with an angry gesture. "These tunnels have to go someplace. Let's go along here until we come to a turning. We can always come back this way if the next tunnel is a dead end or something."

Jo-Beth stumbled after her sister. "I always thought Daddy loved Harry Two the best," she told herself, still surprised at Mary Rose's outburst.

The tunnel they followed divided ahead; Mary Rose went right. The new tunnel twisted and turned. She tried to keep track of all the bends and curves. But what she saw as they entered still another passage drove everything right out of her head. She wanted to scream, but her voice had left her. Jo-Beth caught her breath.

They were in a small room. In the far corner, opposite them, a skeleton was dangling from the roof. Some small breath of air made it appear to be dancing. In front of the skeleton was an old chest.

"I think," Jo-Beth said, and swallowed hard, "I think we've found Dirty Pete."

Mary Rose nodded. "And his gold. That must be the gold Sorehead Jones wanted."

"Shall we look inside and see?"

"Are you crazy or something?" Mary Rose demanded.

"That's what Daddy would do. Daddy would look and see." Jo-Beth was just as terrified as her sister, but she was also bursting

with curiosity. She went over and knelt beside the chest. But no matter how hard she tugged at it, she couldn't get the lid open.

"I'll help." Mary Rose knelt beside her sister. She kept her head down so she wouldn't have to see the skeleton.

The two girls pushed and pulled until at last the lid creaked open. Jo-Beth sat back on her heels.

"Gold! We've found Dirty Pete's gold. Mary Rose. We're rich. We're rich!" Jo-Beth couldn't tear her gaze away from the glittering contents of the chest.

Mary Rose stood up and glanced all around. Which way had they come? How many turns had they taken?

She looked down at her sister. "You know what else, Jo-Beth?" she asked hollowly. "We're also lost."

11

No Way Out

This wasn't daydreaming and pretending. This was real. They were lost in a mine, and Jo-Beth didn't like it at all.

"I'm scared, Mary Rose," she sobbed. "I don't like this place. What good is being rich if you're lost in a place like this, dark and scary and skeletons grinning at you everywhere . . ."

"There's only one skeleton . . ."

"You get me out of here, Mary Rose."

"How am I supposed to do that?" her sister demanded. "Honestly, Jo-Beth. Sometimes you're just too much."

"You're the oldest. You're supposed to take

care of me, and not let me get into trouble or anything. After all," Jo-Beth said, "I'm only seven."

"And a half . . ." Mary Rose began and then stopped talking and listened hard.

"Amigo! We forgot all about Amigo!"

At the far end of the tunnel, the donkey turned his head when he heard his name. He had waited patiently for more jellybeans. When he finally realized he was not going to get any more treats, he had ambled away. Now, with his bells jingling, he began moving steadily onward.

"I'll bet he knows how to get out of here. I'll bet he's been in this mine lots of times with old Doc Peabody. Come on, Jo-Beth." She wiped her sister's tears away with her forefinger. "Don't worry. It'll be all right . . ." She broke off in the middle of her sentence. "What are you *doing*?"

Jo-Beth was stuffing her shirt pocket with a few small pieces of gold-glinting rock from the treasure chest.

"I want to show Daddy these gold rocks. Won't he be surprised when he learns that we found his will-o'-the-wisp?"

"Come *on*! I don't want Amigo to disappear too!"

There was no danger of that. Amigo was in no special hurry. He just bobbed his head up and down and plodded along.

When the girls caught up with the donkey, they patted him and told him what a good boy he was. Amigo nodded, as if he agreed with them, and stopped walking.

"Come on, Amigo," Jo-Beth coaxed.

Amigo hung his head low and stayed where he was.

Mary Rose picked up his rope and tugged. "Push from behind, Jo-Beth. Stubborn old mule," she added as Amigo dug his heels into the tunnel floor.

"I'm tired," Jo-Beth complained after a while. Pushing was hard work. "Why don't we just get on him and try to ride him like a horse?"

"What good will that do?"

"Well, he isn't going anywhere right now," Jo-Beth said, reasonably. "At least we can try something else."

Mary Rose got on first and then helped pull Jo-Beth onto Amigo's back. She held the long rope like a rein. The girls pressed their legs against the donkey, giving him small light kicks and shouting encouragement. To their great surprise, Amigo began to move again.

Mary Rose turned around and grinned at her sister. "This is kind of fun."

Jo-Beth beamed. "I always wanted to ride on a donkey," she declared with great satisfaction.

Mary Rose shook her head. Jo-Beth was back to normal, exaggerating again. How could she have wanted to do any such thing? Mary Rose thought. The girls had never even been close to a donkey before.

It took Amigo only a short while to bring the girls to the entrance of the mine. When

they saw the brightness of the day once more, the girls cheered.

"Okay, Amigo. You can stop now," Mary Rose informed the donkey. But Amigo had his own way of doing things. Back in the mine, he hadn't wanted to start. Here, he didn't want to stop. He just kept on going along the road that led to the town, his feet making small clip-clop noises on the ground, the bells tinkling.

"Where is he taking us?" Jo-Beth cried.

"Where can he take us? The street ends at the jail."

"I don't like donkeys. They don't do anything you want them to." Jo-Beth dug her heels into Amigo's sides. By this time, they had reached the end of the street. For no reason at all, Amigo stopped. The girls jumped off.

"Go back," Jo-Beth said, giving the donkey a push. He looked at her with his soft brown eyes and stayed where he was.

"You know what . . ." Jo-Beth began.

"*Shhh!*" Mary Rose said fiercely. "I thought I heard someone yelling 'Help!'"

The girls listened hard. Both heard the call clearly now. It seemed to be coming from the jail.

"That's Daddy! Come on!"

"What's he doing in there?" Jo-Beth wondered.

"Never mind. We've found him." Mary

Rose dashed into the building, with her sister close on her heels.

"Where have you girls been?" Mr. Onetree demanded resentfully at the same time that both girls said, "Daddy, what are you doing in jail?"

"Just get me out of here. Where have you been?" Without waiting for a reply, he went on, "See if you can find a key in that desk out there. Search the drawers. The man is mad. Do you know how long I've been in this place? If I get my hands on him . . . where have you been all this time? Can't you find the key?"

"What's the matter with Daddy?" Jo-Beth asked in a low voice.

"He's just upset. There isn't any key," she told her father.

"All right. Let's everybody calm down," he said abruptly. "Let me think." The girls watched their father think, but all he seemed to do was pace back and forth. "Did you girls see a man anywhere, dressed as a sheriff . . . ?"

"We didn't see a sheriff," Mary Rose said at once.

"But Doc Peabody took us down into the mine to look for you. He kept calling you Curly," Jo-Beth added.

"Doc Peabody? That was Sourdough Sam. He's not a sheriff and he isn't Doc anybody. He's an old-time Western movie actor . . ." He broke off and glared at his daughters as he realized what they had just told him. "You went into a mine? With a complete stranger?" He was furious. "What in the world is the matter with you, Mary Rose? Haven't you any sense at all?"

Mary Rose's face flushed red. "That's not fair," she thought. "He isn't yelling at Jo-Beth, only at me." She looked away and bit her lip to keep from crying. He hadn't even given her a chance to explain . . .

Mr. Onetree was still talking. "When I think of what could have happened." He shuddered. He pounded his fist on the iron bars of his cell. "I've got to get out of here. There has to be a key. Look again."

There weren't too many places to look, but the girls searched the jail once more. At last Jo-Beth said solemnly, "There just isn't any key, Daddy. How are you going to get out?"

"I can't believe this," Mr. Onetree said. He wrapped his fingers around the bars and looked helplessly at the girls.

And the girls, just as helplessly, stared back at him.

12

And the Wall Came Tumbling Down

"Mary Rose," Jo-Beth begged. "Do something."

Mary Rose was thinking hard. Her father had said something before he had started scolding her . . . what was it? Something about Doc Peabody. He wasn't a sheriff or a doctor. He was a Western movie actor! That was it. Mary Rose's eyes began to shine. She had just had the most wonderful idea.

"Daddy, listen. Can you reach that little window on that back wall?"

"I can push this cot under it. Yes. I expect I can reach it. Why? I've already tried that. The bars won't move."

"Jo-Beth and I are going to get you out, just the way they do it in Westerns. We have a rope. I'll throw it up to you. If you can catch it and tie it around the bars, we can get Amigo to pull the bars loose."

"Just like in the movies." Jo-Beth was delighted. "I've always wanted to do that."

"Who's Amigo?" asked Mr. Onetree, but no one answered because both girls were already running out of the building. Amigo was where they had left him.

Quickly, Mary Rose untied his rope and went to the window.

"Catch, Daddy," she called. Try hard as she could, however, she could not get the rope within her father's grasp.

"That wasn't such a great idea," Jo-Beth observed gloomily. "It's not going to work."

Mary Rose refused to give up. "Get me a rock," she instructed. "Not that one. It's too little. That one," she said as Jo-Beth held another one up for her to approve.

Now, with the rock securely tied at one end

of the rope, it took only six or seven throws before Mr. Onetree caught it. He wrapped the end of the rope around the bars, twisting and knotting it in and out so that it held firmly.

"Okay, Mary Rose. Now what?"

"Be patient, Daddy," she called back. She tied the other end of the rope around the donkey's halter. "Come on, Amigo. Move," she coaxed.

Amigo turned his head and gazed at her, then turned back and stared at the ground. The only thing that moved was his tail, and that was only for a moment.

"I wish we had some jellybeans left," Jo-Beth said.

"Daddy," Mary Rose shouted. "Do you have any jellybeans?"

"*Jellybeans?*"

"Daddy, please. It's very important. Even if you can find only one in your pocket. Please, Daddy. Look."

"Jellybeans," Mr. Onetree muttered. "I

don't believe any of this." Just the same, he searched through his pockets. Sometimes the candy did fall out of the bag. Mrs. Onetree always made sure his pockets were empty before she sent his pants to the cleaners. In between cleanings, however, Mr. Onetree often found stale jellybeans way down at the bottom of his pockets.

In a minute, a green jellybean came flying out the window, followed by a red and then a yellow and finally a black bean.

"That's all I've got." He couldn't see out the window. "And what you expect to do with four jellybeans, I can't imagine," he added.

Jo-Beth had already gathered the candy. "Can I feed him?" she begged her sister.

"You take two and I'll take two. But only give him one bean," Mary Rose warned. "We want him to follow us for the rest."

"Do you think this is going to work?" Suppose it didn't, Jo-Beth thought. How would their father ever get out of the jail?

Jo-Beth held out her hand, so that the donkey could see the candy. "Want a jellybean, Amigo? Come and get it." She backed away quickly as the donkey's tongue darted out for the bean. "Come on, Amigo."

The donkey followed her eagerly. As he trotted after her, the rope tightened. It pulled against the iron bars. It pulled against Amigo. He stopped.

"Give him the jellybean. Quick," Mary Rose urged.

Amigo ate the jellybean with great relish.

"Want more? Come and get it." Again Jo-Beth backed away. This time Amigo didn't even seem to notice the tugging of the rope. He was too busy trying to get at the candy.

Mary Rose watched the bars anxiously. They weren't moving. They weren't moving at all! So much for old Western movies, she thought with deep disappointment.

"You might as well give him the rest of the jellybeans," she told her sister in an unhappy voice. "Me and my big ideas."

"Mary Rose! Look!"

Mary Rose didn't have to be told to look. She couldn't tear her eyes away. The bars hadn't moved. Instead, the whole wall was crashing down.

"Yippee!" Jo-Beth shrieked. She was very good at imagining things, but nothing she had ever imagined was as exciting as this. A whole wall tumbling down, right before her very eyes. And her father stepping through the dust and rubble, laughing, shouting back at her, "Yippee! Yippee ki-ay!"

He put his arms around Mary Rose and kissed her. "You are a forty-day wonder!" he exclaimed.

Jo-Beth beamed. "Do you like Mary Rose now?" she asked.

Mr. Onetree was puzzled. "What do you mean, *now*? I've always liked Mary Rose. I love her. What kind of question is that?"

"Mary Rose told me you don't like her. She says I'm your favorite because you laugh and joke with me."

"I don't have any favorites," Mr. Onetree said at once. He kneeled down so he could look directly into his daughters' faces. "Mary Rose. You're very much like your mother. Do you believe that I like Mommy?"

Mary Rose nodded. "You like her a lot."

"You girls are very different from each other. That doesn't make one better than the other. It just makes you both interesting in different ways. Do you understand that?"

Mary Rose was suddenly quite happy. "Oh, Daddy. I'm so glad."

Mr. Onetree hugged her again. "So am I, honey. So am I."

At that moment, they heard a voice behind them. A tall man was standing and watching them. He looked like Sourdough Sam, except that he was much younger. He had his hands on his hips, and his mouth was tight with anger, his eyes cold and hard.

"What do you people think you're doing?" he demanded. "Don't you know this is private property? How did you get in here anyway?"

Mr. Onetree stood up and stepped in front of the girls.

"I can explain," he said quickly. "You may not believe me, but I really can explain . . ."

13

Everybody Explains

Mr. Onetree talked. And the girls talked. They kept interrupting one another. And so Jo-Beth and Mary Rose learned what had happened to their father while they were gone, while Mr. Onetree grew angrier and angrier when he heard about their adventure in the mine.

"That skeleton is made out of plastic. It's not real," the man who looked like Sourdough Sam said. "And he doesn't have real bullets in his gun. See, the thing is, he takes all the parts in the movie. Did you see him as Dirty Pete?"

The girls shook their heads.

"You mean he didn't put a record on? He always does that."

"Oh," Mary Rose said.

"He should be locked up," Mr. Onetree exploded. "He's a menace."

"I can't do that. Let me explain," the man said.

"I think you'd better." Mr. Onetree wasn't apologetic anymore. Now he was the one with the cold hard look in his eyes.

"My name is George Nicely. That man you want locked up is my father. He used to be a famous actor in Westerns . . ."

"Sourdough Sam. I know. I used to see him in movies every Saturday afternoon when I was a kid. Wait a minute. You said your name is Nicely."

The other man nodded. "My father's real name is Percy Nicely. He wanted to have a name like an old-time cowboy. So he picked Sourdough Sam."

"I don't understand," Mr. Onetree said, "why you just let him wander around . . ."

"It would be cruel to put him away," George Nicely said earnestly. "The thing is, after they finished making the movie, we just bought the set from the company. We own the land. It was the last movie my father ever made. Later on, he got sick. He'd never hurt anybody."

"He locked me up and took the girls down into the mine and scared them."

"He wouldn't have hurt them. I swear. Anyway, I always come over and check up on him. He lives with me in Rock Ridge. That's a little town just beyond the mountain. He walks over here and puts on different costumes."

"He talks to people who aren't there," Jo-Beth informed Mr. Nicely.

"I know. He lives in his own fantasy world. Come to think of it" — Mr. Nicely decided it was now his turn again to be angry — "what are you doing here? This is private property," he reminded them. "If you hadn't come where you had no right to be, none of this would have happened."

"We were lost. And hungry. And tired," Mary Rose told him.

"All we did was follow the sign," Jo-Beth put in helpfully.

"I didn't know that old sign was still up. I'll have to take it down and block off the entrance so no one else will wander in."

"So everything here is all a fake." Jo-Beth was disappointed. "There never was a whispering ghost, was there?"

"Sorry, little lady. The only ghost was in the movie *The Dastardly Murder of Dirty Pete*."

"But we read about the ghost in the paper," Jo-Beth persisted.

"Those were just sent out for publicity, to get critics to write about the movie."

Mary Rose was looking very thoughtful. "There is a ghost here. A real one. Sourdough Sam. He's the ghost of what used to be."

"Mary Rose." Her father shook his head at her.

"No, the little lady is right."

Jo-Beth had a happy thought. "The donkey

is real. And I got to ride on him."

"And the hay in the wagon under the room that wasn't there is real, too. Lucky for me," said Mary Rose.

"I must have forgotten to lock those doors . . ." Mr. Nicely ran his hand through his hair. "When I think what could have happened." He shuddered.

He turned to Mr. Onetree. "I'll just go find Sam. Then I'll pull your car out of the ditch. I've got a heavy chain in my little pickup truck. I want you all to come back to my house and we'll see to it you get a good meal tucked under your belts before you take off. How does that sound?"

"Food," Mary Rose said gratefully. "Real food."

Jo-Beth had been very quiet while the others had been talking. Now she took the rocks from her shirt pocket and held them out. Her face was sad. "Then we didn't find Dirty Pete's skeleton, did we? And I guess this isn't real gold either."

Mr. Nicely smiled down at her. "You have to keep in mind where you are," he told her gently. "That's the gold they used in the movie — Dirty Pete's gold, remember? Only it's no more real than anything else around here. It's called fool's gold."

"I like it. Whenever I look at it, I'll think of this place," Mary Rose said.

"Me, too," said Jo-Beth. She put the rock in her pocket. "Please, can we go now? I'm starved!"

14

Never Follow
a Creepy Sign

Jo-Beth sat well back in the seat of the car. She knew they had been in the "ghost town" only a short time, but it felt as if days and days had gone by. They had had a hearty meal at Mr. Nicely's house. Their car had been taken care of, and Mr. Nicely had given Harry Onetree careful directions on how to get back on the main highway.

"I feel sorry for Sam," Mary Rose said suddenly. "It must be terrible not to know what's real and what isn't." She turned around in her seat in the front of the car and stared at her sister.

Jo-Beth stared back in alarm. Something in her sister's manner frightened her.

"What's the matter with you?" she demanded when Mary Rose continued to look at her without speaking.

"All right, Mary Rose," Harry Onetree said patiently. "What's bothering you?"

"It's Jo-Beth. She's always making believe and pretending. I don't think she ought to do it anymore, Daddy. I think it's dangerous."

Jo-Beth wailed. "Am I going to turn into a Sourdough Sam?" Her eyes filled with tears. "Daddy! I don't want to be a Sam."

"Relax," Mr. Onetree said. "There's nothing wrong with daydreaming. We all do a little daydreaming now and then. Maybe some of us more than others." He looked into his rear-view mirror at his younger daughter. "As a matter of fact, Jo-Beth, your imagination is part of your personality. It makes you interesting, and fun to be with."

"And a pain in the neck a lot of times, too,"

Mary Rose grumbled, giving her father a side-long glance. Maybe he wouldn't like her saying that.

"And a pain in the neck sometimes," Harry Onetree agreed. He reached out and squeezed Mary Rose's hand and smiled at her. It gave Mary Rose a lovely warm feeling that spread all through her body. Her father liked her. He really and truly did like her.

"The most important thing to remember, when you're daydreaming, Jo-Beth," he continued, "is that you *know* that's what you're doing. Just keep that in mind and you have nothing to worry about."

Mary Rose sighed with relief. She didn't want anything to happen to her sister. Jo-Beth sank back into her seat, busy with her thoughts. If she hadn't spotted the sign on the road, none of this would have happened. They probably would have been well on the way to reaching Grandmother Onetree's house.

Noticing how quiet Jo-Beth had become,

and believing that his younger daughter was still thinking about Sam living in his fantasy world, Mr. Onetree asked, "Do you understand what I've been telling you? What have we learned from our adventure?"

Both he and Mary Rose expected Jo-Beth to say that she would try to cut down on her daydreaming. Instead, she said promptly, and didn't mind one bit when they laughed, "Never follow a creepy sign."

Secretly, she was glad that they did.

120